The Secret of
ST. NICHOLAS

By Ellen Nibali

Illustrated by Lon Eric Craven

Fairland Books
West Friendship, MD

For Jennifer, Ben, and Vince
— and their children

Note to parents and teachers:
St. Nicholas was bishop of Myra, Lycia (present day Turkey) in the fourth century. This story is inspired by an episode recorded by the biographer, Simeon Metaphrastes, in the tenth century, and by the message in the Gospel of Matthew 6:4 — Keep your deeds of mercy secret, and your Father who sees in secret will repay you.

The history of Santa Claus is many centuries long. It encompasses miracles and myths, cultures and politics, flights of fancy and commercial schemes, but it began with St. Nicholas. The author chose this episode because it is key to who St. Nicholas was. Of all the stories about St. Nicholas, scholars suspect this one is actually true.

For children's questions about Santa Claus, this story inspires with a real man and his heroic deeds. It also traces the connection between Jesus and Santa Claus traditions of today.

The Secret of St. Nicholas by Ellen Nibali
Illustrated by Lon Eric Craven

Library of Congress Control Number: 2008904810

(Summary: The orphan boy Nicholas tries to save three girls from slavery.)
[1. Christmas—Fiction. 2. Saints—Fiction. 3. Slavery—Fiction.
4. St. Nicholas—Fiction. 5. Middle East—Fiction.]
ISBN- 978-0-9818154-1-1

Copyright 2008 by Ellen Cook Nibali
Printed and bound in the United States of America

To order additional copies, please go to: www.fairlandbooks.com

Fairland Books
P.O. Box 63
West Friendship, MD 21794

LONG AGO when Christmas was new, there was no St. Nicholas. Most people had never even heard of Christmas.

But in a warm land near a great blue sea, a boy named Nicholas knew the Christmas story. That was not enough for Nicholas.

"Tell me more about Christmas, the night of wonders," Nicholas begged his father and mother.

They told how a star showed the way and angels appeared announcing the birth of Jesus. Shepherds hastened from their fields and wise men traveled from afar to worship the newborn king.

"But," said his father, "instead of a royal palace, they found a stable full of animals. Instead of a rich prince on a throne, they found the holy babe sleeping in a manger."

"In a feed trough?" Nicholas laughed. "God surprised everyone!"

Nicholas decided that God liked surprises. When Jesus grew up, he never stopped surprising people. Jesus even said, "Do good deeds in secret."

Now it happened that Nicholas' father and mother both died. They left Nicholas three bags of gold. Nicholas hid the gold for safekeeping.

Then out he went to earn his own way in the world.

His village harbor was a bustling place. Brave little fishing boats sailed out to catch their daily harvest of fish. Fat merchant ships jostled to load cargos of silk and spice. Sometimes the dreaded slave ship came, taking people away never to be seen again.

Nicholas found work on a fishing boat, flinging out nets in search of slippery silver fish.

On his way to the harbor each day, Nicholas passed
by the home of a nobleman and his three daughters.
The nobleman's house cracked and crumbled
about him, but still he dressed grandly
and entertained as though he had not
a care in the world.

One morning the nobleman's youngest daughter was hanging her wash to dry at the window. Big tears rolled down her cheeks and plopped onto her freshly washed stockings.

"Your stockings will never dry that way," said Nicholas.
"Oh, Nicholas," the daughter cried. "Our last gold coin is spent. Tomorrow Father takes my oldest sister to the slave ship to sell her for gold, or else we shall all starve."

Nicholas dashed home and took out his three bags of gold. "Two bags are plenty for me," he said.

He was about to take one to the nobleman, when he remembered these words of Jesus: Do good deeds in secret. So instead, Nicholas made a plan.

That night while the village slept, Nicholas crept through the dark and winding streets to the nobleman's house. In a flash, he tossed the heavy bag through the open window. He listened for it to land with a thud, but all he could hear was the nobleman snoring.

The next morning the youngest daughter went to fetch her dry stockings. "How heavy this stocking is," she said. "What a curious shape is the toe." She reached down inside. "Gold!"

Her cry woke the village from end to end. Villagers sprang into the streets, arguing over the mysterious bag of gold.

"A trick!" "A mistake!" "A miracle!" they exclaimed.

Nicholas laughed. "Perhaps it is a gift."

"What does it matter?" the nobleman cried. "There is money for us to live and pay for three marriage dowries besides. Now my three splendid daughters can be married."

Indeed the oldest daughter soon married a fine young man. Nicholas danced with joy at the wedding feast. Meanwhile, the nobleman let the gold coins slip through his fingers like water.

One afternoon Nicholas spied the slave ship entering the harbor. "What brings them back so soon?" he said angrily.

"Shame, shame," hissed an old fisherwoman. "The nobleman's gold is gone again. Tomorrow he sells his middle daughter to the slavers."

"If I give my second bag of gold," Nicholas thought, "only one bag will remain. One bag is still enough for me."

When night fell Nicholas crept to the nobleman's house, where a new row of freshly washed stockings hung drying. Eyes twinkling, carefully he aimed and — swish, into a stocking dropped the second bag of gold.

At once a lamp flared. "We're saved!" cried the sisters when they saw the jiggling, sagging stocking.

The nobleman rushed to the window and peered as hard as he could into the night, but there was no one to be seen.

Before long Nicholas was singing merrily at the wedding of the middle daughter. "Surely the nobleman learned his lesson this time," thought Nicholas. "The second bag of gold should last as long as he lives."

One day a storm approached the village. Wind whipped and waves crashed. Nicholas hurried to tend his fishing nets.

There he met the youngest daughter crying. "Those must be tears of joy,"
Nicholas hollered over the wind, "for soon you will be wed."
The daughter shook her head.

"Then surely the salt wind stings your eyes," he said. "What else could possibly make you cry?"

The daughter pointed. There in the harbor waited the slave ship. The nobleman's gold was gone again.

That night Nicholas poured out his third bag of gold. None remained. "Without my gold, what will become of me?" he wondered.

Though the night was dark and his candle weak, a coin caught the light. To Nicholas, it sparkled like the wondrous star that once led the way to a humble stable.

And with that,
Nicholas knew
what he would do.
   Nicholas raced
the sun to the
nobleman's
window. Freshly
washed stockings
hung in a row.
Quickly he aimed
and tossed his last
bag of gold.

He missed!
With a crash and a clatter, gold coins scattered everywhere.
Nicholas turned to run, but someone grabbed him from behind.

"Now I've got you!" his captor cried.

Like a mighty fish trapped in a fisherman's net, Nicholas twisted this way and that, but he could not escape.

"Nicholas," exclaimed the nobleman. "So it is you!"

"Let me go," said Nicholas. "The sun is almost up."

"Wait," cried the nobleman. "I have been a fool and worse. I will beg my daughters' forgiveness and mend my ways. But first, I must thank you. You are a hero."

"I didn't do it to be a hero or to be thanked," said Nicholas.

"How can I repay you?" said the nobleman. "I know — I will tell everyone it was you!"

Nicholas laughed. "Keep my secret for as long as you live, and that will be enough."

The nobleman promised.

This time the nobleman loved his daughters more than his gold, living out his days in simple contentment. True to his word, he did not tell Nicholas' secret, even when he thought he would burst from keeping it.

Years went by and the old nobleman lay dying. "For so long," he told his weeping daughters, "I have kept the secret of the mysterious bags of gold, but I can keep it no longer."
With his final breath he said, "Nicholas."

From person to person the secret flew, over desert and over sea, until Nicholas' secret wasn't a secret anymore.

As for Nicholas, he grew to be a great and holy man. So beloved was he that he was given a special name: Saint Nicholas.

Stories say that with God's help St. Nicholas did many brave and marvelous deeds:

He saved sailors from sinking in a storm.

He stopped the beheading of an innocent man.

He found food when famine threatened his people.

Perhaps best of all were the three good deeds he did in secret. For on Christmas, the birthday of Jesus, boys and girls all over the world rush to see what new good deeds were done in the night. And that began with a boy named Nicholas and his three bags of gold.